For loving mothers everywhere

THIS IS A BORZOI BOOK PUBLISHED BY ALFRED A. KNOPF

Copyright © 2017 by Maggie Smith

All rights reserved. Published in the United States by Alfred A. Knopf, an imprint of Random House Children's Books,
a division of Penguin Random House LLC, New York.

Knopf, Borzoi Books, and the colophon are registered trademarks of Penguin Random House LLC.

Visit us on the Web! randomhousekids.com

Educators and librarians, for a variety of teaching tools, visit us at RHTeachersLibrarians.com

Library of Congress Cataloging-in-Publication Data is available upon request.
ISBN 978-0-553-51019-5 (trade) — ISBN 978-0-553-51020-1 (lib. bdg.) — ISBN 978-553-51021-8 (ebook)

The illustrations in this book were created using watercolor and acrylic paints on multi-media board.

MANUFACTURED IN CHINA
January 2017   10 9 8 7 6 5 4 3 2 1   First Edition

And I Have You

A BOOK OF MOTHERS AND BABIES

MAGGIE SMITH

Alfred A. Knopf · New York

A cat has her kittens,

a dog has her puppies,

a sheep has her lamb,

and I have you.

A hen has her chicks,

a duck has her ducklings,

a cow has her calf,

and I have you.

Wherever you go and whatever you see,

I'll always have you

and you'll always have me.

A rabbit has her bunnies,

a fox has her kits,

a deer has her fawn,

and I have you.

A pig has her piglets,

a goat has her kids,

a horse has her foal,

and I have you.

Wherever you go and whatever you do,

you'll always have me

and I'll always have you.